P9-DFW-159

Poems have Roots

Books by Lilian Moore

Papa Albert

I Feel the Same Way

I Thought I Heard the City

Sam's Place

See My Lovely Poison Ivy

To See the World Afresh
(Compiled by Lilian Moore and Judith Thurman)

Think of Shadows

Something new begins . . .

I'll Meet You at the Cucumbers

Don't Be Afraid, Amanda

Adam Mouse's Book of Poems

I Never Did That Before

Poems Have Roots

Poems have Roots

New Poems by
Lilian Moore

Illustrations by Tad Hills

J
811
M

A Jean Karl Book
Atheneum Books for Young Readers

LAKEWOOD MEMORIAL LIBRARY
LAKEWOOD, NEW YORK 14750

FOR DICK, JONATHAN, AND GERMAN—
ALWAYS THERE WHEN I NEEDED THEM

Atheneum Books for Young Readers
An imprint of Simon & Schuster Children's Publishing Division
1230 Avenue of the Americas
New York, New York 10020

Text copyright © 1997 by Lilian Moore
Illustrations copyright © 1997 by Tad Hills

All rights reserved including the right of reproduction in whole or in part
in any form.

Book design by Lee Wade

The text of this book is set in Bernhard Modern.
The woodcut-style illustrations are rendered in Adobe Photoshop 3.0.5.

First Edition
Printed in the United States of America
10 9 8 7 6 5 4 3 2 1

Library of Congress Cataloging-in-Publication Data
Moore, Lilian.
Poems have roots : new poems / by Lilian Moore.—1st ed.
p.   cm.
"A Jean Karl book."
Summary: A collection of poems that explores the wonders of nature,
including "Waterfall," "Maple Talk," "Snow Dust," and "If a Deer
Dreamed."
ISBN 0-689-80029-0
1. Children's poetry—American. [1. Nature—Poetry. 2. American poetry.]
I. Title.
PS3563.O622P63   1997
811'.54—dc21
96-47456

CONTENTS

IN THE THEATER OF THE SKY

The sun's going down
with a great hurrah,
a gold ball
sinking,
staining the sky.

The sun's half down
in a sky aflame.
Colors splash and stream—
nothing's the same!

Only the rim of the
sun
still glows—

   going

     glowing

       gone.

*2

LAKEWOOD MEMORIAL LIBRARY
LAKEWOOD, NEW YORK 14750

"New show tomorrow!"
the weather people cry.
"See a battle
of clouds!
A spectacular
fray!
No admission to pay
in the theater of the sky!"

Shell,
so cleverly curled,
sing me a sea song!

Tell me tales
of dolphins
cavorting   of
great whales snorting,
bright fish
flashing
their scales.

What song do you bring
to me, Shell?

Only this—
for all who live
in the waters
of the
world,
I sing of their longing,
"Unpoison the sea!"

5

WATERFALL

*W*inter breathed on the
waterfall   stilled it
left ragged icicles
hanging from the rocks.

Through short dark days and
long dark nights
we missed the chatter,
the rollicking spill.

Warm winds came   uncurling
leaves on maple trees,
forsythia glowed
like lights turned on.

Still
the waterfall
hung silent
in tattered ice.

We waited.

We heard it
today   the joyous rush,
saw water leaping again
over rocks,

spraying sunlight,
announcing
the news:
"*Now* it's spring!"

THE AUTOMATED BIRD WATCHER

"*I*nformation Please!
  What's all the
  pull and push
  going on in that
  berry bush?"

Operator:
  To see the nest
  the robin made
  Press One
  To see the clutch of
  eggs she laid
  (all three sky blue)
  Press Two
  To see three small
  mouths open wide,
  Mother Bird
  stuffing food inside

Press Three

 If now you feel

 some urgency

 about the

 empty nest

Press Emergency

 To watch new robins

 on the lawn,

 tugging worms

 with baby brawn.

MAPLE TALK

Plant us.
Let our roots go
deeply down.
We'll hold the soil
when rain tugs
at the earth.

Plant us.
You will better know
how seasons come
and go.

Watch for
    our leaves unfurling
    in spring green,

our leafy roofs of summer
over pools of shade,

our sunset red and gold
igniting autumn's blaze.

When cold winds
leave us bare
we'll show you treetop nests
where songbirds hid
their young.

And when
in early spring
the sweet sap flows again,
have syrup for your pancakes!

Plant us.

ISLAND RISING IN THE SEA

A crack opens
    in a volcano
        under the sea.

The volcano roars
    rages
        spews fiery ash.

Hot lava
    piles high
        ever higher
spreads,

And slowly an island
    rises
        in the sea.

Slowly
lava hardens
into rock.

Slowly sea waves
grind rock into
sand.

Sun heat and
rain chill split
rock into soil.

The new island
waits now
for wind and waves
to bring

seeds of life
from
other shores.

FROGS ARE DISAPPEARING

The song sparrow is trilling
an aria.
The tree swallow is warbling
alto notes.
That's woodpecker drumming.
But where is the deep rumble
of the bass?

Where are the frogs?

Where are the frogs that lived
in this pond, greeting each other
with endless croaks?
      the small frogs plopping
      back into the water,
      evading the eager children?

the majestic bullfrog,
sunning himself on the
wet rocks, ready for any
princess and her
magic?

Who ever thought
we'd miss the
raucous frog talk, the
throaty bellows,
the nightly clamor?

The frogs are
gone   and
the silence is eerie.

THE WETTER, THE BETTER

*O*f all the days in that
long July
  of endless blue in cloudless sky
  of grass burned brown
  earth cracks in the creek
everything thirsting
everything dry,

the day I remember
began with a growl,
a thundery roar,
then a drummer's tattoo
on rooftop and pane.

We dashed out the door
to hug
the rain

to run on grass
that was drinking
its fill

to hear the creek gurgle
its faint new
spill

to splash and to spin
wet to the skin,
the wetter, the better
the very much wetter, the
very much better.

Of all the days in that
long July
                    I remember—
                    who could forget?—
that glorious day
when our world was
wet.

LOVE AFFAIR

The clouds
must love these hills.

Wind-driven
they flee to the
hill's embrace.

Drifting   lingering
they wrap cloud scarfs
like hugs
around the hills.

Slowly,
dark and moist,
they come to the
thirsty hills

and keep them green.

IF YOU LIVE
WHERE THERE
ARE HILLS

*F*ull moon tonight.

We watch the moon rise
behind the hill,
moving as if
from a deep and secret place.

A slice of moon
peers
over the hill.

then rising steadily
            its perfect face
            flushed with borrowed
            sun

the moon sails
off the hilltop
into the night sky

and pours
its dazzling glow
on the darkened world below.

"Look!" we cry.
"Look at our shadows!
It's bright as day!"

PILGRIM FLOWER

They left the
unfriendly shores
of home

crossed a
strange sea to
a strange land

carrying memories
pots and pans and
hopes

and the white flower
they called
Queen Anne's lace.

The flower too
took root in the
new soil.

It fills our
meadows now   like
summer snow,

stands patient, tall
on our dusty
country roads

as if waiting
to bow to a
phantom queen

passing in a
royal phantom
coach.

CONVERSATION

"How noble it is
to fly!"
said the woodchuck
to the wren.
"How elegant you look
in the sky!"

"How safe you look
on the ground!"
said the wren
in reply.

"Safe!" said the woodchuck.
"I dare not roam.
I scurry
to my burrow
at every strange sound!"

"Ah yes,"
said the wren.
"Prowlers abound!
I must worry
lest my nest be found."

Then woodchuck and
wren said, "Good-bye"—
each with a sigh

for those
who burrow
and those
who fly.

LAKEWOOD MEMORIAL LIBRARY
LAKEWOOD, NEW YORK 14750

SNOW DUST

Snow dust is
falling
lightly,
brushing in

new shapes
upon
old places.

Windows
on sudden ledges
are whitely framed.
(Were all those edges
really there before?)

Briskly,
steps emerge
in front of
houses

and now   above each door
long-forgotten
arches

wear
jaunty
sailor hats.

It's a new
snow-painted
street.

WHERE I LIVE IT NEVER SNOWS

I think about
snow that I have

never seen.

I know skis can skim
and sleds can

race

on snowy hills.

I know snow sports
are played
with forts   and
snowballs whizzing.

I know snowmen in
clown face stand
in yards, watching

children
make angel wings.

Some things
I
know.

But how does it
feel
       to lift your face to
       falling snow?

How does it
taste
       if you let your tongue
       explore?

What is it like—
       the quietness of
       snow
       that can hush
       a city's roar?

THE TREE
IN THE TUB

The tree in the tub wore
silver
like other Christmas trees

and stars and
winking lights.

It too breathed
peppermint   gathered
ribboned boxes of
surprises
around itself
and like other trees,
glowed
window magic
in the winter night.

Now
the lights are
out on all the trees

and in the chilly streets
they lie   tinsel
tangled in dry needles,
waiting
beside other finished things.

The tree in the tub
still stands
in the window,
piney and
green and
alive.

IF A DEER
DREAMED

I. The Deer

*T*hree shadows in the
winter twilight—
a buck, a doe, and a fawn.

They have come out
of the snowy woods,
remembering apples.

Now in the old orchard
they move from tree to
tree, pawing the snow.

There are no apples.

Somewhere a twig snaps.
They are off, bounding
back to the woods

white tails lifted,
streaks in the
fading light.

Hungry,
they lie down to rest,
to sleep.

Does one of them dream?
Could it be a dream
like this?

II. The Dream

*T*he buck wants the
doe and the fawn to
come with him.

He has something to show them.

He doesn't know what it
is but he urges them
out of the woods.

He hurries them to the
orchard, to trees
deep in new snow.

He waits   watching
the trees. Suddenly small
green buds appear.

Yes, this is what he wanted
to show them.

The leaf buds open,
pink blossoms drift
down on the fresh snow.

Now there are tiny green
apples on the branches.
The apples turn red.

They grow bigger.
The apple-heavy boughs hang
lower and lower.

Now even the fawn can reach them.

A RIVER DOESN'T
HAVE TO DIE

A river rises in the
mountains, from a lake called
Tear of the Cloud.
Tears and clouds.
The river knows them well.
It has shared every mood
of the sky.
It has plunged through waterfalls,
rapids, wooded highlands
and gorges.
This river was old when
Henry Hudson first saw
its restless waters surging
out to the ocean
he had crossed.

This river has flowed through
history.
It has borne the canoes of
Mohicans and Senecas
and the ships of explorers
from a distant world.
Cannon smoke misted its waters
when a new nation
battled for freedom
on its banks.

Thick with life, the river
nourished the towns
and cities
that grew on its shores.
How did it come to pass that
they turned their backs on their
river—saw it as a carrier
of waste?

Rubble poured into its waters,
raw sewage, chemicals—
an endless cargo. Not even fish
could breathe.
The river was dying.

Those who loved the river
mourned.

Like a curtain drawing back,
a four-year drought
lowered the waters
revealed the old cars rusting
in muck, the massive garbage—
the river's true agony.

Those who loved the river
found their voices.

Fishermen, poets, scientists,
children, people of the town
worked to save the river,
began to write, to sing, to tell
how the river ran through their lives,
their voices heard, until at last, a new
    law said:
            "The waters of this river
            must be clean again."

Slowly, the wounded river healed.
The piney mountains gathered rain
to wash and fill its banks.
The striped bass left its eggs
once more in the cattails.
And children swim again in the clear
    waters of the river.
A river doesn't have to die.

SOME NOTES

In the Theater of the Sky

My picture window in Seattle is a front seat at the Theater of the Sky. The snow-capped Olympic Mountains are like a backdrop for magical sunsets—the kind that artists and poets are forever trying to catch. They say here in the Northwest: "Wait five minutes and the weather will change." So there is a constantly changing choreography of clouds as well.

Waterfall

There are sudden scenic waterfalls throughout the Hudson Valley in New York State. The one in this poem was a special, modest waterfall that I passed often, driving across the Shawangunk Mountains from the village of Kerhonkson where I lived to the town of New Paltz. This waterfall was like a personal calendar—independent and reliable—announcing in its own good time frost in the fall and thaw in the spring.

The Automated Bird Watcher

A telephone call I made to an automated office phone offered me *ten* choices I could press! I got lost on the way, muttering "Where will it all end?" This poem, of course, was just for fun.

Maple Talk

When the days begin to warm up, though the nights are cool, in spring the sap begins to flow in the sugar maples and black maples; then the sugaring begins. One sees the buckets on the trees catching the sweet sap dripping. Later the sap is boiled down to a syrup—a sweetener used long ago by the Native Americans and the pilgrims, and still the way to make a pancake special!

Frogs Are Disappearing

No one is quite sure why, but even in the protected environment of Yellowstone National Park, frogs and toads have been disappearing. Drought? Acid rain? Chemical pollution? Trout that eat eggs and tadpoles? Researchers are trying to unravel the mystery.

The pond in this poem, on a farm where I lived, will never seem quite the same without the frogs.

Love Affair

One is always aware of the low and intimate hills in Berkeley, California. And the clouds do seem to be on comfortable terms with the hills. When I lived there, we always welcomed them, especially after a dry spell when the hills were turning brown. Once, after a long walk, with the hills ever present and the clouds clinging affectionately to them, this poem emerged.

If You Live Where There Are Hills

It's the same glorious full moon wherever you live, of course. But rising from behind the low Shawangunk Mountains in upstate New York, the full moon was always mysterious, brilliant, and a surprise. Sometimes, as in this case, it seems to take years of watching before there is a poem. This poem, too, rose slowly from some secret place.

Snow Dust

It doesn't often snow in Seattle, and after living in the Northeast, I find the snow that does come very gentle. Watching it outline steps and doors and ledges, it is easy to think of this snow dusting as snow painting. The same day that I watched this gentle snowfall, I read of a blizzard in the East that brought back memories of snowstorms that buried cars. There is snow—and there is *snow!*

The Tree in the Tub

This poem has very long roots. The Christmas

tree I remember best from childhood was a tree in a tub in the house across the street. What a surprise—and a revelation—it was to see it green and alive after the holidays!

If a Deer Dreamed
This poem was adapted from a manuscript called *Animal Dreams* by Sam Reavin, and is dedicated to his memory.

A River Doesn't Have to Die
I rejoiced at the news, as printed in the *New York Times,* that the Hudson River has been reclaimed, that once again it holds fish to catch and water to drink. I lived for many years near this magnificent river, mourning its decay and adding my voice to the struggle to save it.

The lake—Tear of the Cloud—where the river rises is on Mt. Marcy in the Adirondack Mountains in New York State. The river flows for more than three hundred miles on its journey to the sea. The drought referred to in the poem occurred from 1962 to 1966.

So polluted was the river that students in a crosstown bus before reaching a tributary would make bets on the color of the water, because a dyeing plant upstream kept them guessing.

It was said that children in the town of

Beacon, swimming in the polluted waters, never dunked their heads in the water and so never learned to dive.

That a three-hundred-mile sewer could once more pulse with life is an epic happening. I hope there will be many poems and songs to tell the story of this beautiful river that didn't have to die.

3 2005 0176171 2

J 811 M
Moore, Lilian.
    Poems have roots

15.00

APR 1 3 1998	DATE DUE	
AUG 0 2 2004		
MAY 2 1 2005		
SEP 0 6 2005		

LAKEWOOD MEMORIAL LIBRARY
12 W. Summit Street
Lakewood, New York 14750

WITHDRAWN

Member of
Chautauqua-Cattaraugus Library System